A BOX CAN BE MANY THINGS

By Dana Meachen Rau

Illustrated by Paige Billin-Frye

SCHOLASTIC INC.

New York   Toronto   London   Auckland   Sydney
Mexico City   New Delhi   Hong Kong   Buenos Aires

For my brother,
Derek **-D. M. R.**

To Marty,
Brennan,
and James
who like
boxes, too
-P. B-F.

Reading Consultant
LINDA CORNWELL
Learning Resource Consultant
Indiana Department
of Education

ISBN 0-516-24197-4

15 14 13 12   11/0

Printed in China   62

First Scholastic printing, October 2002

"This box is junk,"
Mom says.

3

"A box can be many things,"
I say.

The box is a cave.
I am a bear.

"Stay out!" I growl.

We flip the box over.

The box is a car.

"Vroooom!"
we shout.

We punch holes in the sides.

The box is a house.

"Come visit!" I say.

We rip more holes.

The box is a cage.

"Tweet!"
my pet brother sings.

We tear the box more.

"Now the box is junk,"
my brother says.

"No it's not," I say.

The box
is a hat
and a flag
and a necklace
and a sword.

A box can be
many things.

Word List (51 words)

a	flip	my	sides
am	growl	necklace	sings
and	hat	no	stay
be	holes	not	sword
bear	house	now	tear
box	I	out	the
brother	in	over	things
cage	is	pet	this
can	it's	punch	tweet
car	junk	rip	visit
cave	many	say	vroooom
come	Mom	says	we
flag	more	shout	

About the Author

When Dana Meachen Rau was little, she and her brother always used their imaginations. They pretended their beds were pirate ships, and the hallway was a bowling alley. But the best creation of all was setting up the boxes in the basement to look like a palace! Dana works as a children's book editor and has also authored many books for children. She lives with her husband, Chris, and her son, Charlie, in Farmington, Connecticut, where she still imagines she lives in a palace.

About the Illustrator

Paige Billin-Frye lives in a neighborhood filled with kids in Washington D.C., with her husband, two sons, one cat, several fish, and lots of flowers in her garden.